The Adventures of Onyx
and

The Far Side of the Lakes

by Tyler Benson

Ensign Benson Books LLC

Illustrations by David Geister
Design by Joe Fahey

Ensign Benson Books LLC
PO BOX 609
Gloucester, VA 23061
www.adventuresofonyx.com
ensignbensonbooks@gmail.com

Printed and bound in the United States of America

First Edition

10 9 8 7 6 5 4 3 2

LCCN 2015952883

ISBN 978-0-9892846-6-0

This book was expertly produced by Book Bridge Press.
www.bookbridgepress.com

To my son Parker. You are a reminder that as life leaves this world, new life is also born. Always remember those who came before you, appreciate your time with those who are with you now, and work to make this world a better place for those to come. Let the adventures continue!

Love, Dad

U.S. COAST GUARD
216

"Hold on!" Captain Stevens yelled over the howl of the north wind.

The U.S. Coast Guard Cutter *Alder*'s bow plunged deep beneath the dark water and disappeared into the lake. Spray hit the bridge windows and nothing could be seen but white, then turquoise, then darkness. Like a roller coaster reaching the bottom of its first descent, the cutter leveled out and its hull moaned from the weight of the water pressing against it. Then as quickly as the *Alder* dipped down into the back of a wave, it burst upward toward the sky!

"Here we go again. Hold on!" called out Captain Stevens.

"I think I am going to be sick," Hogan said to Onyx.

"Welcome to Lake Superior!" the captain yelled to Hogan and Onyx. "Welcome to the far side of the Great Lakes."

The captain looked out across the turbulent waves and said, "Today we set sail to remember the *Edmund Fitzgerald*."

US COAST

Hogan, Onyx, and Captain Stevens stood on the bridge of the cutter *Alder* watching the waves break over the railing. The waves rocked the cutter back and forth, making the ship's bell ring violently.

"We are almost there, shipmates. We are almost there," Captain Stevens said reassuringly.

"I don't know how much more of this I can take," Hogan said. "It looks like Lake Superior is even getting to Onyx today. She looks seasick!"

Onyx let out an uncomfortable bark as she tried to rest on the *Alder*'s bridge deck.

Captain Stevens patted Onyx on the head and said to Hogan, "Today you join us on temporary assigned duty to cross the big lake from Duluth, Minnesota, to Whitefish Bay. We are facing freezing rains and the gales of November to remember the loss of the twenty-nine sailors of the SS *Edmund Fitzgerald*."

"Captain, can you tell us the story of the *Edmund Fitzgerald?"* Hogan asked.

Captain Stevens paused, then looked out the window and pointed to the horizon. "There, right there in that very spot, the largest American freighter on the Great Lakes sank. It happened forty years ago this evening on November 10, 1975, in a Lake Superior storm very much like this one."

Onyx looked up, barely able to lift her head. She looked out the bridge window and then at the captain. Hogan and Onyx could see in the captain's eyes and hear in his voice the respect he had for the power of Lake Superior.

EDMUND FITZGERALD

"It's time, follow me," the captain said.

An announcement was made from the bridge throughout the cutter for the crew to report to the aft deck.

Hogan started to follow the captain, but Onyx didn't move. Hogan kneeled down beside her. "You really are seasick, aren't you, girl?" He could feel Onyx trembling. He tried to lift her to her feet but she was too weak. "Don't worry, girl, I'll carry you."

Hogan was weak from his own seasickness, but he picked Onyx up and carried her below to the aft deck.

When Hogan arrived on the aft deck, he found the majority of the *Alder*'s crew lined up and standing in formation.

The freezing rain fell, and the cold water of Lake Superior struck their faces. Hogan quickly carried Onyx to the front of the formation and took his place among his shipmates. He set Onyx down on the deck next to him. With a mighty effort, Onyx slowly stood up. The crew could see that she was weak, but was trying to be strong.

Hogan looked concerned. "You don't have to be out here, girl," he told Onyx. "I can take you back inside."

Onyx whined back. Hogan could tell that she wanted to be involved, she wanted to be with him, and seasickness was not going to stand in her way.

U.S.
GUARD

"Attention on deck!" one of the chiefs called out, and the crew quickly popped to attention.

Captain Stevens stood in front of them. "Thank you for joining me, shipmates," he announced. "Today we remember the *Edmund Fitzgerald*, which tragically sank in this very spot forty years ago in a violent storm. On her final voyage, the *Edmund Fitzgerald* had a crew of twenty-nine sailors that consisted of the captain, the first, second, and third mates, five engineers, three oilers, a cook, a wiper, two maintenance men, three watchmen, three deckhands, three wheelsmen, two porters, a cadet, and a steward." The captain paused, and the crew stood motionless despite the freezing rain. "No survivors were ever found," he said more quietly. "But they are not forgotten. For on this anniversary, we continue an annual memorial for the fortieth time. We will ring our ceremonial bell and read the names of the crewmen, then we will take a moment of silence to commemorate all lives lost on the Great Lakes."

Captain Stevens waved to two shipmates to bring over the bell.

Hogan watched, but he was worried about Onyx. "Onyx, you look worse," he said. "I'm really worried about you!" Hogan could see in her eyes that she was using all the strength she had to stand there next to him. She was shaking even worse than before.

The captain called out, "We remember the twenty-nine souls of the *Edmund Fitzgerald* and all lives lost on the Great Lakes."

The two shipmates began to chime the bell until it rang twenty-nine times, once for each man on the *Edmund Fitzgerald.* With each chime, the shipmates called out a name.

Onyx could barely stand, but she listened to every chime and to every name. By the twentieth chime, she was shaking so badly that Hogan kneeled down to pick her up. "That is it, girl. We're going back inside the cutter!" But Onyx refused. Then, as the shipmates read the final name and gave the twenty-ninth chime, Onyx collapsed to the deck.

EDMUND
FITZGERALD

"Onyx!" Hogan yelled.

The crew quickly gathered around the miracle dog, who was in and out of consciousness. Hogan began to check Onyx. The captain pushed through the crewmen. Hogan looked up at Captain Stevens. "She's really sick, Captain," he said, "and she needs help."

"Not to worry, shipmate," the captain said. "I'm requesting a medical evacuation. A Coast Guard helicopter from Traverse City is in the area for training, and I can get it here quickly." The captain said to his crew, "Let's get ready for helo ops. Let's get ready for a medevac. Let's get our miracle dog some help!"

With a united, "Aye, aye!" the crew took their positions.

Through the wind, the rain, and the darkness, a bright orange Coast Guard helicopter appeared. The helicopter flew two circles around the cutter and then hovered over the *Alder*'s stern.

"You're going to be okay, girl," Hogan said. Onyx whimpered as Hogan tried to calm her.

The helicopter's spotlight shone down and a trail line was dropped to the cutter's deck. The crew quickly grabbed the line and brought the rescue basket down to the deck.

Hogan wrapped Onyx in a blanket. "Don't worry, girl, we're getting you help," he said.

The captain returned from the bridge. "Okay, it's time to go!" he yelled over the wind and the rain. "You take good care of Onyx. Take good care of our miracle dog!"

Hogan saluted the captain. "Thank you for doing this, Captain."

Captain Stevens smiled and patted Hogan on the back and then pointed to the rescue basket.

Hogan picked Onyx up and ran to the rescue basket. Two shipmates held the basket on deck as Hogan climbed in, holding Onyx tightly against him. The shipmates gave the helicopter a thumbs-up, and Hogan and Onyx were lifted into the sky.

When the rescue basket reached the helicopter's door, Hogan was met by two familiar faces. "Sinclair! Shaw! Am I glad to see you!"

Shaw pulled the basket into the helicopter and shut the door and Sinclair helped Hogan climb out. Sinclair handed Hogan a communication headset so he could talk to the flight crew.

"She's really sick," Hogan said. "I've never seen her like this before. She needs help."

A familiar voice came over the headset. "Well, you brought her to the right place. You brought her to the Angels in the Air!" Hogan looked toward the cockpit as one of the pilots looked back. "Pelkey!" Hogan yelled over the headset.

Pelkey smiled and said, "Hold on tight. Station St. Ignace has been notified and is ready for us. We'll be there soon."

Hogan smiled and gave Pelkey a thumbs-up and then turned to Sinclair, who was checking Onyx over with his hands on her side. He looked at Hogan with a surprised look on his face and said to the flight crew, "We need to get there as fast as this helicopter will fly."

The rain started to let up and the storm began to pass. Hogan, Onyx, and the Angels in the Air were soon over the Straits of Mackinac and Station St. Ignace.

As the helicopter landed on Station St. Ignace's helicopter pad, Dean and Evans ran from the station to the helicopter, and Captain Waters and Remi ran over from the cutter *Biscayne Bay*.

The helicopter powered down and the cabin door opened. Out stepped Sinclair holding Onyx in his arms, as Hogan stepped out behind him holding something else in a blanket.

U.S. COAST GUARD

EVANS

Dean looked worried. He stepped forward and asked, “Is she okay? What’s the matter with Onyx?”

Sinclair and Hogan kneeled down next to Remi as he nuzzled up against Onyx.

Hogan smiled up at his shipmates and said, “Onyx is just fine. In fact, she is better than fine. She is a mother!” Then Hogan pulled the blanket back to reveal two tiny puppies sleeping under his arms. “Onyx wasn’t seasick,” he said. “She was pregnant.” Hogan looked at Remi and said, “It appears you and Onyx are now parents.”

Remi barked and wagged his tail. Onyx licked Remi’s face.

Remi laid down next to Onyx as she licked and nuzzled her puppies. The Guardians of the Straits and the Angels in the Air gathered around.

"So what are their names?" Evans asked.

Hogan said, "Well, since the puppies were born in a search and rescue helicopter, I thought it was only appropriate that we should call this little guy Search and this little gal Rescue."

Onyx and Remi both barked in agreement.

Dean nodded and said, "Search and Rescue, huh? I like that!"

The storm had passed and the rising moon shone down on the new family. All was perfect and peaceful. Onyx and her shipmates started their day remembering lives lost on the Great Lakes, but they ended it with the reminder that new lives are also born on the Great Lakes.

Onyx looked down at her puppies. She had completed another Coast Guard adventure, an adventure on the Far Side of the Great Lakes. But her greatest adventure had just begun—her adventure as a mother to her puppies, Search and Rescue.

GREAT LAKES AUTHOR **Tyler Benson** is from St. Louis, Michigan. He has served in the United States Coast Guard for more than a decade in St. Ignace, Michigan. He began writing short stories about his search and rescue adventures in the Coast Guard to educate his four young children about what Daddy does when he goes on duty for 48 hours at a time. He wanted them to learn the importance of service to their country and helping those in need. To help them better understand his job, Tyler wrote the stories featuring his station's morale dog, Onyx. These stories soon evolved into a dream—to publish a book series that would serve as a tribute and a way to bring recognition to all who serve or have served in the United States Coast Guard.

PHOTO BY SHOOT FOR FIVE PHOTOGRAPHY

The Far Side of the Lakes is Tyler's seventh book in the successful Adventures of Onyx series. Let the adventures continue!

www.adventuresofonyx.com